For Gray, Trey, Logan, Heidi,
Finley, Suzanna, Oliver, Hattie,
Shepherd and baby Jade

Your presence in my life is one of God's greatest gifts.

With Love,
Bama

In loving memory of Ozzie Wambolt
who lived and loved to entertain
May 5, 2020

www.mascotbooks.com

For more information, please contact:
Mascot Books
620 Herndon Parkway, Suite 320
Herndon, VA 20170
info@mascotbooks.com

Library of Congress Control Number: 2020910479

CPSIA Code: PRT0920A
ISBN-13: 978-1-64543-451-1

Printed in the United States

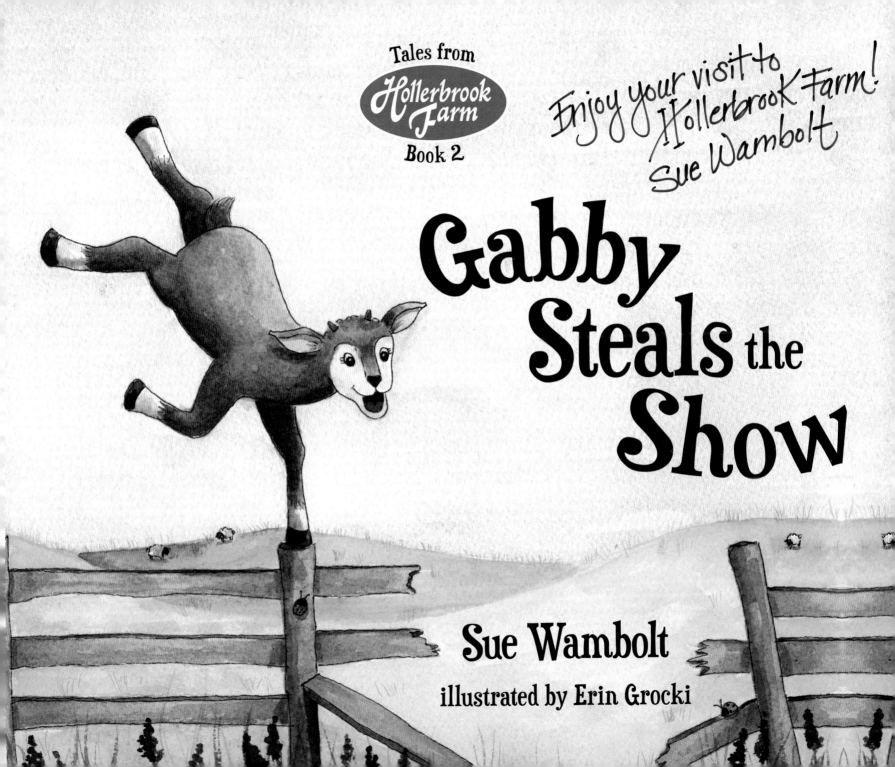

Tales from
Hollerbrook Farm
Book 2

Enjoy your visit to Hollerbrook Farm!
Sue Wambolt

Gabby Steals the Show

Sue Wambolt

illustrated by Erin Grocki

If some things in this story do not make sense
like bites out of trees and the broken fence,
then perhaps you might want to read about Pete,
one of the hungriest pigs you will ever meet.
He even ate more than big Joe the cow,
but where do you think ole Pete is now?
Read *Pete the Hungry Pig* to get the backstory
and to see Pete's appetite in all of its glory.

Down a long, windy road in the town of Ash River
was the unusual farm of old Owen McShiver.
Nestled in a valley with long sprawling views,
the perfect setting for an afternoon snooze.
On Hollerbrook Farm life was peaceful and slow.
Things were quite easy for Owen and Flo.

The entrance was lined with big apple trees,
branches bursting with apples that swayed in the breeze.
If you followed the drive up the hill you would see,
past the barn and the meadows and an old oak tree,
a little white house that was simple and quaint
though in need of some fixin' and a fresh coat of paint.

From the long farmer's porch, you could see far and wide,
past the barn and the fields and the broad countryside.
And off in the distance on a clear, sunny day,
trains could be seen chug-chugging away...
Up over the mountains, the faint whistles would blow
as trains headed out with the County Fair show!

Hollerbrook Farm was home to Owen and Flo,
to Breeze the horse, and a cow named Joe.
There was Ned the sheep and his brother, Jed,
a goat named Rose, and her husband, Fred.
And then there was Gabby, the newest goat on the farm—
she was cute as a button and bursting with charm.
Life, it was quiet, and the days, they were lazy,
until things with Gabby got a little bit crazy!

One late afternoon as Owen sat sipping tea,
he saw something silly (I'm sure you'd agree).
For as Breeze trotted around on the field of green clover,
Gabby jumped on his back—over and over!

She imagined herself performing in front of a crowd,
so with every dismount, she stood and she bowed.
But Breeze was old and was not having fun;
he just wanted to roam quietly and graze in the sun.

Now he'd had enough of the goat's circus tricks,
so he gave his hind legs a few strong and swift kicks.
In the blink of an eye, Gabby flew through the air;
first one flip, then two—she spun without care.

She landed, *ker-plunk,* in a pile of hay
then jumped to her feet and sauntered away.
But Gabby the goat had more tricks up her sleeve.
More trouble was brewing—you just wouldn't believe!

It was a well-known fact in the town of Ash River
that the tastiest apples were grown by Owen McShiver.
So yummy, you see, that they won first prize
when baked into Flo's famous mouth-watering pies.

While Flo walked to the mailbox one late afternoon
just strolling along, whistling a tune...
she happened to see Gabby in the apple trees
swinging on the branches like a flying trapeze!
Can you imagine Flo's surprise?
She truly could not believe her eyes!
With every sway, apples fell to the ground—
all bumping and bruising and rolling around.

Mushy apples lay squished beneath the trees,
their sweetness attracting swarms of hungry bees
who chased poor Gabby all around the farm,
saving Flo's yummy apples from all further harm.
Not only was Gabby a nuisance to sweet old Breeze,
but she bruised the apples and angered the bees.
And just when it seemed that she could do no more harm,
Gabby stirred up even more trouble on Hollerbrook Farm.

At night when the barn animals went to sleep
with the pigs and cows and horses and sheep,
Gabby the goat just wanted to play—
imagining herself performing in a famous ballet!

She jumped onto the fence on a moonlit night
while the crickets chirped and the stars shone bright.
She tiptoed across the creaky old fence and then,
struck a pose on the post and went back again!

But the rickety old fence made such a racket
that Owen jumped out of bed and threw on his jacket.
Night after night, he returned Gabby to bed,
as visions of cheering crowds danced in her head.
Owen was tired of being kept awake—
he just wanted to sleep for goodness' sake!

Things on Hollerbrook Farm were a bit out of whack,
from the problems with Breeze and his poor aching back,
to the piles of apples which fell and were bruising,
to the nighttime antics that kept Owen from snoozing.
Everyone was starting to get a bit crabby
thanks to the shenanigans of a goat named Gabby.

It just so happened that Owen and Flo
won front row seats to the circus show
for Flo's blue-ribbon pies that were beyond compare
which she entered in a contest at the county fair.
And goodness knows it wouldn't do any harm
for Owen and Flo to get away from the farm.
So they hopped in the truck without looking back
and headed to town with a *clickety-clack!*

Crowds from all over poured into the tent.
For the small town of Ash River, it was quite an event!

OLLIE
the EXTRAORDINARY ORANGUTAN

FEARLESS FINLEY
and ELLIE the ELEPHANT

HATTIE'S HIGH FLYING TRICKS

GRAY the GREAT
LION TAMER

Not a seat was empty; the big top was packed
as everyone waited patiently for the first circus act.
A tall man on stilts walked around the big top
selling popcorn and peanuts and cold soda pop!
Music started playing and the audience cheered
as the circus march began and the ringmaster appeared.

From jugglers to acrobats to wild animals in cages, it was great fun for everyone—folks of all ages.

There were clowns in go-carts darting to and fro, honking and waving and stealing the show!

Ellie THE ELEPHANT

Silly SUZANNA the TRAMPOLINE TUMBLER

The ringmaster took his spot in the center of the tent
excited to announce the main event:
"Ladies and gentlemen," he hollered as the lights dimmed low.
"Please turn your attention to the high wire show."

Up on the platform twenty feet in the air
Owen thought he was seeing things, or was it the glare?
For tightrope walking across the high wire with ease,
then soaring across the tent on a flying trapeze,
was Gabby the goat in a leotard and all
just swinging away—she was having a ball!

Back and forth, Gabby swung across the big top.
First one flip, then two—she did not want to stop!
What in the world? Owen couldn't believe his eyes.
Seeing Gabby in the circus was quite a surprise.

The crowd rose to their feet; the applause sure was loud,
and Owen had to admit that he felt rather proud.
Gabby was a star—she had performed like a pro,
so the ringmaster invited her to be a part of the show
as they entertained audiences in towns far and wide,
past long sprawling farms and the vast mountainside.

Owen thought about the problems with Breeze the horse,
and the nights Gabby was out on the fence, of course.
And Flo thought about her apples and delicious pies
that had won her blue ribbons and this circus prize.
They looked at one another, and deep down they knew
that Gabby was a performer through and through.
She had spent her life practicing for this big day
and even took the risk as a stowaway,
to perform as an acrobat on the flying trapeze
and cross the high wire with the greatest of ease.

Owen and Flo watched as the Big Top came down
and the circus prepared to head out of town.
The clowns and the jugglers and the funny tall man
all found their places in the long caravan.

In the blink of an eye, they were off and away
after what could be called an unusual day.
And as the last of the wagons came rolling by,
something in the distance caught Owen's eye.

For way up on the top of the tiger's cage
was Gabby the goat on her own private stage!
Twirling and spinning and in all her glory,
ready to start a new chapter in her own circus story.

With thanks for

Roberta's amazing pies!